Soil for Our Garden

by Judy Kentor Schmauss

HOUGHTON MIFFLIN HARCOURT

PHOTOGRAPHY CREDITS: (c) ©Marnie Burkhart/Fancy/Corbis; 3 (b) ©Terry Vine/Blend Images/Corbis; 4 (b) ©Ashley Cooper/Encyclopedia/Corbis; 5 Photodisc/Getty Images; 7 (br) ©JupiterImages/Thinkstock/Alamy; 10 (t) ©Ocean/Corbis; 11 (tr) ©Marnie Burkhart/Fancy/Corbis

ISBN: 978-0-544-07232-9

13 14 15 16 0940 20 19 18 17

4500693646   A B C D E F G

Contents

Vocabulary	Stretch Vocabulary
soil	moisture
clay	texture
silt	gritty
sand	space
property	

Introduction

Mrs. Reed's class wants to grow some tomatoes. The clerk at the garden store tells Mrs. Reed that some plants grow best in certain kinds of soil. He asks Mrs. Reed about the soil at the school. Mrs. Reed doesn't know. But she knows how to find out!

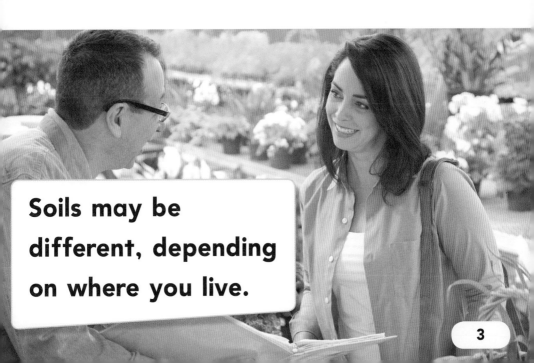

Soils may be different, depending on where you live.

Clay, Silt, and Sand

The class looks on the Internet. They find that all soil has tiny bits of rock in it.

Clay soil has the tiniest bits of rock. Clay holds a lot of moisture, or water. It makes mud when it's very wet. It gets hard and cracks when it's very dry. If you roll wet clay into a ball, it will stay that way.

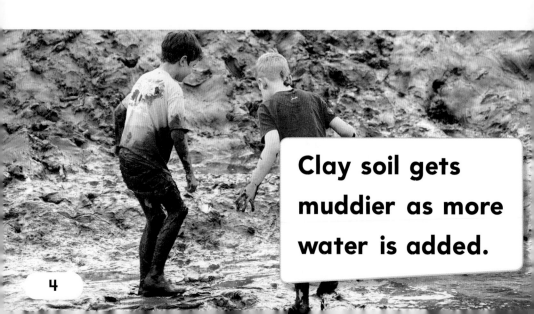

Clay soil gets muddier as more water is added.

Silt has bigger bits of rock than clay does. The bits are still tiny, though. They are smaller than the bits in sand.

Silt runs through your fingers. You cannot roll it into a ball.

Sandy soil is made up of small bits of rock. The bits are bigger than the ones in silt or clay. You can roll sandy soil into a ball. Then it falls apart.

Many garden soils have silt, sand, and clay.

The Properties of Soil

The children in Mrs. Reed's class read about other soil properties besides the size of soil's tiny bits of rock.

Color is another property. Clay makes a soil dark. Sand and silt make soils that are lighter in color.

Different soils have different textures. Texture is how something feels.

Scientists say there are about 170 different colors of soil.

The children investigate different types of soil. The first one is thick, heavy, and sticky when wet. This soil with clay would make good mud pies!

The next one feels gritty. It feels like salt. This soil is sandy.

The third soil feels smooth and slippery. Silt gives soil this silky feeling.

Both salt and soil with sand feel gritty.

Soil and Space

The children discover that soil with clay has the least space between its rocks. Air and water do not get through the tiny bits of rock easily. This makes it hard for plants to grow.

	clay soil	sandy soil
Size of rocks	can barely be seen	can see individual rocks
Color	wet: dark brown dry: medium to light brown	medium to light brown
Texture	wet: sticky and heavy dry: dusty	gritty

Sandy soils have more space between the tiny bits of rock. The spaces let the air in, but water and food drain out more easily.

When soil is silty, there is more space between the bits of rock, but not too much. Air and water can get between the tiny bits but do not run through too quickly. Silty soil is quite easy to shovel and work with in a garden.

These soils came from two different gardens.

silt

sand

The Importance of Studying Soil

We eat carrot roots.

For plants to grow well, the plants need air, water, and food. Some plants need more water than others. Some plants grow under the ground. They have to be able to push down through the soil. The soil has to be just right.

The children in Mrs. Reed's class find out that their soil is silty. Since silt holds water but doesn't cause puddles, tomatoes are a good choice.

Tomatoes grow well in silty soil.

Mrs. Reed was right! She knew her class would find out what they needed to know about soil.

Sample the Soil

Dig up a few tablespoons of soil from three different places around your school. Compare the color and texture of each sample. Use a hand lens to look at the size of the bits of rock in each sample. Make a chart and record your findings.

 Write About It

Suppose you write a gardening advice column for your local newspaper. Write a letter to someone who would like information about sandy soil.